For this story's journey, thanks to
Liz Bicknell, Jane Yolen, and the
Willard/Andrews and Korinek families
C. L. S.

Text copyright © 2000 by Carole Lexa Schaefer
Illustrations copyright © 2000 by Stan Fellows

First edition 2000

Library of Congress Cataloging-in-Publication Data
Schaefer, Carole Lexa. The copper tin cup / Carole Lexa Schaefer;
illustrated by Stan Fellows. —1st ed.
p.   cm.
Summary: A young boy enjoys drinking cocoa from a special cup
that has been passed down through several generations of his family.
ISBN 0-7636-0471-2
[1. Family life—Fiction. 2. Heirlooms—Fiction. 3. Drinking cup—Fiction.]
I. Fellows, Stanley, date, ill. II. Title.
PZ7.S3315Co   2000
97-46488   [E]—dc21

2 4 6 8 10 9 7 5 3 1

Printed in Hong Kong

This book was typeset in Bernhard Modern.
The illustrations were done in watercolor.

Candlewick Press
2067 Massachusetts Avenue
Cambridge, Massachusetts 02140

The Copper Tin Cup

Carole Lexa Schaefer

illustrated by
Stan Fellows

CANDLEWICK PRESS
CAMBRIDGE, MASSACHUSETTS

Sammy Carl drinks cocoa
from his favorite cup, a cup
made of copper and tin.
It is a cup that cannot break.
The handle, which fits just
right in Sammy Carl's hand,
ends in a curlicue snail.

On one side of the cup,
just below the smooth worn
place on the rim, there are
two finely carved letters.
Sammy Carl traces
them with a finger.
"S for Sammy.
C for Carl," he says.
"My name, my cup."
And it is. But Sammy
Carl knows that the cup
was not always his.

When Sammy Carl's mama
was a little girl, she sipped
lemonade from it at parties
for her dolls in the garden
on summer afternoons.

Afterwards, she washed the
cup herself, then dried it
with a soft checkered towel
until the letters gleamed.
"S for Samantha.
C for Caroline.
My name, my cup," she said.
And she was right.
But she knew that the cup
had not always been hers.

Before, it had belonged to her papa,
Sammy Carl's grandpa. As a boy, he lifted
it off its hook in the old blue cupboard and
ran out to the barn with it in the morning.

He set it next to the milking pail

under Hedda the cow. Some squirts

of warm milk splattered right into

the copper tin cup. *Ping-ka-ting-plash*.

He rubbed droplets of milk off

the letters.

"S for Sam.

C for Charles.

My name, my cup," he said.

And that was so.

But first the cup had belonged to Grandpa's big sister, Sammy Carl's great-aunt Serena. She drank precious fresh water from it during the long sea journey to the family's new home.

Before going to sleep each

night, she held the cup

close and read the letters

with her fingers in the dark.

"S for Serena.

C for Carlotta.

My name, my cup,"

she whispered.

And it was true.

The cup was made for her by her parents, Sammy Carl's great-grandpapa Samuel and great-grandmama Carla.

After the cup cooled, Carla, an engraver, etched in the letters: S and C.

Samuel, a coppersmith, hammered bright copper into the curved cup shape. Then he lined it with a layer of hot melted tin.

They gave the cup to Serena.

Serena Carlotta's cup.

Sam Charles's cup.

Samantha Caroline's cup.

Sammy Carl's cup.

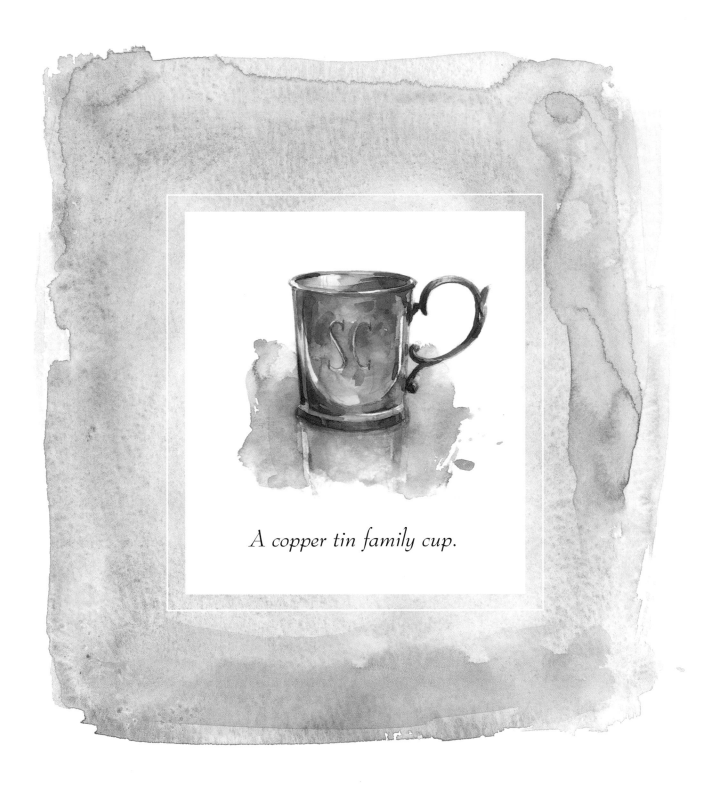

A copper tin family cup.

Sammy Carl sits in the winter

moonlight and traces the letters

again. Mama sits down beside him.

He looks at her, then at the cup.

"Want to taste my cocoa?" he says.

"I sure do," she says, and takes a sip.

"Mmm, delicious."

"Yep," says Sammy Carl.

   He takes a sip too.

"Cocoa tastes best in our cup."